AF230131

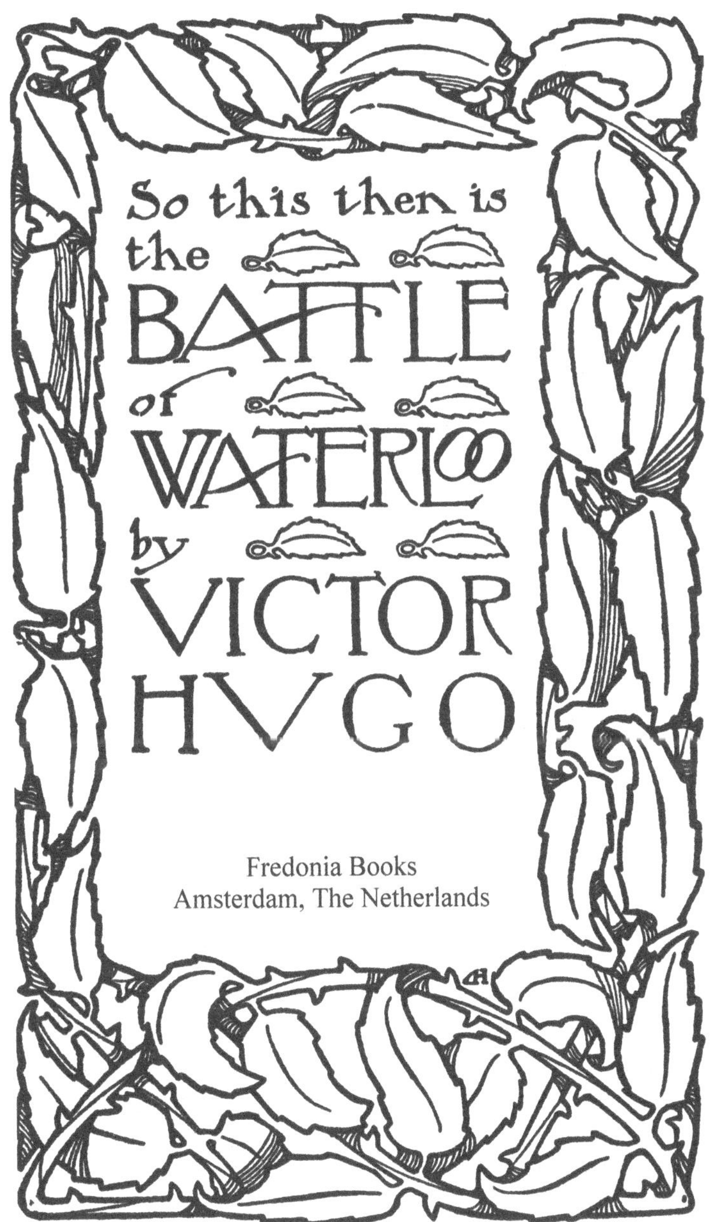

Fredonia Books
Amsterdam, The Netherlands

Battle of Waterloo

by
Victor Hugo

ISBN 1-58963-234-6

Reprinted from the 1907 edition

Fredonia Books
Amsterdam, The Netherlands
http://www.fredoniabooks.com

In order to make original editions of historical works available to scholars at an economical price, this facsimile of the original edition of 1907 is reproduced from the best available copy and has been digitally enhanced to improve legibility, but the text remains unaltered to retain historical authenticity.

WATERLOO

Waterloo

Byron

THERE was a sound of revelry by night,
And Belgium's capital had gathered there
Her Beauty and her Chivalry, and bright
The lamps shone o'er fair women and brave men;
A thousand hearts beat happily; and when
Music arose with its voluptuous swell,
Soft eyes looked love to eyes which spake again,
And all went merry as a marriage-bell;
But hush! hark! a deep sound strikes like a rising knell!

Did ye not hear it?—No; 't was but the wind,
Or the car rattling o'er the stony street;
On with the dance! let joy be unconfined;
No sleep till morn, when Youth & Pleasure meet
To chase the glowing Hours with flying feet—
But, hark!—that heavy sound breaks in once more
As if the clouds its echo would repeat;
And nearer, clearer, deadlier than before!
Arm! Arm! it is—it is—the cannon's opening roar!

Within a windowed niche of that high hall
Sate Brunswick's fated chieftain; he did
    hear
That sound the first amidst the festival,
And caught its tone with Death's prophetic
    ear.
And when they smiled because he deemed
    it near,
His heart more truly knew that peal too
    well
Which stretched his father on a bloody
    bier,
And roused the vengeance blood alone could
    quell:
He rushed into the field, and, foremost fighting,
    fell.

Ah! then and there was hurrying to and
    fro,
And gathering tears, and tremblings of dis-
    tress,
And cheeks all pale, which but an hour ago
Blushed at the praise of their own loveliness;
And there were sudden partings, such as
    press
The life from out young hearts, and choking
    sighs
Which ne'er might be repeated; who could
    guess
If ever more should meet those mutual eyes,
Since upon night so sweet such awful morn
    could rise!

And there was mounting in hot haste: the
    steed,
The mustering squadron, and the clattering
    car,
Went pouring forward with impetuous
    speed,
And swiftly forming in the ranks of war;
And the deep thunder peal on peal afar;
And near, the beat of the alarming drum
Roused up the soldier ere the morning
    star;
While thronged the citizens with terror
    dumb,
Or whispering, with white lips—"The foe!
    They come! they come!"

And wild and high the "Cameron's gather-
    ing" rose!
The war-note of Lochiel, which Albyn's
    hills
Have heard, and heard, too, have her Saxon
    foes :—
How in the noon of night that pibroch
    thrills,
Savage and shrill! But with the breath
    which fills
Their mountain-pipe, so fill the mountain-
    eers
With the fierce native daring which instils
The stirring memory of a thousand years,
And Evan's, Donald's fame rings in each clans-
    man's ears!

iii

And Ardennes waves above them her green
    leaves,
Dewy with nature's tear-drops, as they
    pass,
Grieving, if aught inanimate e'er grieves,
Over the unreturning brave,—alas!
Ere evening to be trodden like the grass
Which now beneath them, but above shall
    grow
In its next verdure, when this fiery mass
Of living valor, rolling on the foe
And burning with high hope, shall moulder
    cold and low.

LAST noon beheld them full of lusty life,
  Last eve in Beauty's circle proudly gay,
  The midnight brought the signal-sound of
    strife,
  The morn the marshalling in arms, — the
    day
Battle's magnificently-stern array!
The thunder-clouds close o'er it, which
    when rent
The earth is covered thick with other clay,
Which her own clay shall cover, heaped
    and pent,
Rider and horse,—friend, foe,—in one red burial
    blent!

THE BATTLE OF WATERLOO

On The Nivelles Road

 FINE May morning of 1861, a wayfarer, the person who is telling this story, was coming from Nivelles and was proceeding toward La Hulpe. He was on foot and following, between two rows of trees, a wide paved road which undulates over a constant succession of hills, that raise the road and let it fall again, and form, as it were, enormous waves ❧ He had passed Lillois & Bois-Seigneur Isaac, and noticed in the west the slate-covered steeple of Braine l'Alleud, which looks like an over-turned vase ❧ He had just left behind him a wood upon a hill, and at the angle of a cross-road, by the side of a sort of worm-eaten gallows which bore the in-scription, "Old barrier, No. 4," a wine-shop, having on its front the following notice ❧ "The four winds, Echabeau, private coffee-house."

About half a mile beyond this pot-house he reached a small valley, in which there

"

is a stream that runs through an arch
formed in the causeway ❧ The clump of
trees, wide-spread but very green, which
fills the valley on one side of the road,
is scattered on the other over the fields,
& runs gracefully & capriciously toward
Braine l'Alleud. On the right, and skirting
the road, were an inn, a four-wheeled
cart in front of the door, a large bundle
of hop poles, a plough, a pile of dry shrubs
near a quick-set hedge, lime smoking in
a square hole, and a ladder lying along
an old shed with straw partitions ❧ A
girl was hoeing in a field, where a large
yellow bill—probably of a show at some
Kermesse—was flying in the wind ❧ At
the corner of the inn, a badly paved path
ran into the bushes by the side of a pond,
on which a flotilla of ducks was naviga-
ting. The wayfarer turned into this path.
❡ After proceeding about one hundred
yards, along a wall of the fifteenth century, surmounted by a coping of crossed
bricks, he found himself in front of a large
arched stone gate, with a rectangular
moulding, in the stern style of Louis
XIV., supported by two flat medallions.
A severe facade was over this gate : a
8

wall perpendicular to the facade almost joined the gate and flanked it at a right angle ঌ On the grass-plot in front of the gate lay three harrows, through which the May flowers were growing pell-mell. The gate was closed by means of two decrepit folding doors, ornamented by an old rusty hammer.

The sun was delightful, and the branches made that gentle May rustling, which seems to come from nests even more than from the wind. A little bird, probably in love, was singing with all its might. The wayfarer stooped and looked at a rather large circular excavation in the stone to the right of the gate, which resembled a sphere. At this moment the gates opened and a peasant woman came out. She saw the wayfarer and noticed what he was looking at.

"It was a French cannon-ball that made it," she said, and then added: "What you see higher up there, on the gate near a nail, is the hole of a heavy shell, which did not penetrate the wood."

"What is the name of this place?" the wayfarer asked.

"Hougomont," said the woman.

The wayfarer drew himself up, he walked a few steps, and then looked over the hedge ❧ He could see on the horizon through the trees a species of mound, and on this mound something which, at a distance, resembled a lion ❧ He was on the battle-field of Waterloo.

Hougomont

THIS estate was a mournful spot, the beginning of the obstacle, the first resistance which that great woodman of Europe, called Napoleon, encountered at Waterloo; the first knot under the axe-blade. It was a chateau, and is now but a farm. For the antiquarian Hougomont is Hugo-mons; it was built by Hugo, Sire de Sommeril, the same who endowed the sixth chapelry of the abbey of Villers. The wayfarer pushed open the door, elbowed an old caleche under a porch, & entered a yard. The first thing that struck him in this enclosure was a gate of the sixteenth

10

century, which now resembles an arcade, as all has fallen around it. A monumental aspect frequently springs up from ruins. Near the arcade there is another gateway in the wall, with key-stones in the style of Henri IV., through which can be seen the trees of an orchard ❧ By the side of this gateway a dunghill, mattocks, and shovels, a few carts, an old well with its stone slab and iron windlass, a frisking colt, a turkey displaying its tail, a chapel surmounted by a little belfry, and a blossoming pear tree growing in espalier along the chapel wall,—such is this yard, the conquest of which was a dream of Napoleon's ❧ This nook of earth, had he been able to take it, would probably have given him the world. Chickens are scattering the dust there with their beaks, and you hear a growl,—it is a large dog, which shows its teeth and fills the place of the English ❧ The English were admirable here; Cooke's four companies of guards resisted at this spot for seven hours the obstinate attack of an army.

Hougomont, seen on a map, buildings & enclosures included, presents an irregular quadrangle, of which one angle has been

broken off. In this angle is the southern
gate, within point-blank range of this
wall ✖ Hougomont has two gates, the
southern one, which belongs to the chateau, and the northern which belongs to
the farm. Napoleon sent against Hougomont his brother Jerome; Guilleminot's,
Foy's, & Bachelie's divisions were hurled
at it; nearly the whole of Reille's corps
was employed there and failed; and Kellerman's cannon-balls rebounded from
this heroic wall. Bauduin's brigade was
not strong enough to force Hougomont
on the north, and Soye's brigade could
only attack it on the south without
carrying it.

The farm buildings border the court-yard
on the south, and a piece of the northern
gate, broken by the French, hangs from
the wall. It consists of four planks nailed
on two cross beams, and the scars of the
attack may still be distinguished upon it.
The northern gate, which was broken
down by the French, and in which a
piece has been let in to replace the panel
hanging to the wall, stands, half open, at
the extremity of the yard; it is cut square
in a wall which is stone at the bottom,

brick at the top, which closes the yard on the north side ✦ It is a simple gate, such as may be seen in all farm-yards, with two large folding doors made of rustic planks; beyond it are fields. The dispute for this entrance was furious; for a long time all sorts of marks of bloody hands could be seen on the side-post of the gate, and it was here that Bauduin fell. The storm of the fight still lurks in the court-yard: horror is visible there; the incidents of the fearful struggle are petrified in it; people are living and dying in it,—it was only yesterday. The walls are in the pangs of death, the stones fall, the breaches cry out, the holes are wounds, the bent and quivering trees seem making an effort to fly.

This yard was more built upon in 1815 than it is now; buildings which have since been removed, formed in it redans and angles ✦ The English barricaded themselves in it; the French penetrated but could not hold their ground there. By the side of the chapel stands a wing of the chateau, the sole relic left of the manor of Hougomont, in ruins, we might almost say gutted ✦ The chateau was employed as a keep, the chapel served as a block-house ❧ Men exterminated each other there. The French, fired upon from all sides, from behind walls, from granaries, from cellars, from every window, from every air-hole, from every crack in the stone, brought up fascines, and set fire to the walls and men; the musketry fire was replied to by arson.

In the ruined wing you can look through windows defended by iron bars, into the dismantled rooms of a brick building; the English guards were ambuscaded in these rooms, and the spiral staircase, hollowed out from ground-floor to roof, appears like the interior of a broken shell. The staircase has two landings; the English, besieged on this landing and massed on the upper stairs, broke away the lowest ❧ They are large slabs of blue stone which form a pile among the nettles. A dozen steps still hold to the wall; on the first the image of a trident is carved, and these inaccessible steps are solidly set in their bed ❧ All the rest resemble a toothless jaw. There are two trees here, one of them dead, and the other, which was wounded on the foot, grows green again in April. Since 1815 it has taken to growing through the stair-case ✄ ✄ ✄

Men massacred each other in the chapel, and the interior which is grown quiet again, is strange ✄ Mass has not been said in it since the carnage, but the altar has been left—an altar of coarse wood supported by a foundation of rough stone ✄ Four whitewashed walls, a door opposite the altar, two small arched windows, a large wooden crucifix over the door, above the crucifix a square air-hole stopped up with hay; in a corner, on the ground, an old window sash, with the panes all broken,—such is the chapel. Near the altar is a wooden statue of St. Anne, belonging to the fifteenth century; the head of the infant Saviour has been carried away by a shot ✄ The French, masters for a moment of the chapel and then dislodged, set fire to it ✄ The flames filled the building, and it became a furnace; the door burnt, the flooring burnt, but the wooden Christ was not burnt; the fire nibbled away the feet, of which only the blackened stumps can now be seen, and then stopped. It was a miracle, say the country people ᨳ The walls are covered with inscriptions. Near the feet of Christ you read the name Henquinez; then these others, Conde de Rio Maior, Marquis y Marquisa de Almagro (Habana) ᨳ There are French names with marks of admiration, signs of anger. The wall was whitewashed again in 1849, for the nations insulted each other upon it. It was at the door of this chapel that a body was picked up, holding an axe in its hand; it was the body of sub-lieutenant Legros ᨳ ᨳ ᨳ

On leaving the chapel you see a well on your left hand. As there are two wells in this yard, you ask yourself why this one has no bucket and windlass? Because water is no longer drawn from it. Why is it not drawn? Because it is full of skeletons. The last man who drew water from this well was a man called Willem van Kylsom: he was a peasant who lived at Hougomont, and was gardener there. On June 18, 1815, his family took to flight and concealed themselves in the woods. The forest round the abbey of Villers sheltered for several days and nights the dispersed luckless country people. Even

16

at the present day certain vestiges, such as old burnt trunks of trees, mark the spot of these poor encampments among the thickets ﹆ Willem van Kylsom remained at Hougomont "to take care of the chateau," and concealed himself in a cellar. The English discovered him there; he was dragged from his lurking-place, and the frightened man was forced by blows with the flat of a sabre to wait on the combatants. They were thirsty, and this Willem brought them drink, and it was from this well he drew the water. Many drank there for the last time, and this well, from which so many dead men drank, was destined to die too. After the action, the corpses were hastily interred; death has a way of its own of harrassing victory, and it causes pestilence to follow glory ﹆ Typhus is an annex of triumph. This well was deep and was converted into a tomb. Three hundred dead were thrown into it, perhaps with too much haste ﹆ Were they all dead? the legend says no. And it seems that, on the night following the burial, weak voices were heard calling from the well.

This well is isolated in the centre of the

yard; three walls, half of brick, half of stone, folded like the leaves of a screen, and forming a square tower, surround it on three sides, while the fourth is open. The back wall has a sort of a shapeless peep-hole, probably made by a shell. This tower once had a roof of which only the beams remain, and the iron braces of the right-hand wall form a cross. You bend over and look down into a deep brick cylinder full of gloom ❧ All round the well the lower part of the wall is hidden by nettles ❧ This well has not in front of it the large blue slab usually seen at all Belgian wells ❧ Instead of it, there is a frame-work, supporting five or six shapeless logs of knotted wood which resemble large bones. There is no bucket, chain, or windlass remaining: but there is still the stone trough, at which the horses were watered ❧ The rain-water collects in it, and from time to time a bird comes from the neighboring forest to drink from it and then fly away.

One house in this ruin, the farm-house, is still inhabited, and the door of this house opens on the yard. By the side of a pretty Gothic lock on this gate there is an iron handle. At the moment when the Hanoverian lieutenant Wilda seized this handle in order to take shelter in the farm, a French sapper cut off his hand with a blow of his axe. The old gardener Van Kylsom, who has long been dead, was grandfather of the family which now occupies the house. A grey-headed woman said to me: "I was here, I was three years old, and my sister, who was older, felt frightened and cried ❧ I was carried away to the woods in my mother's arms, and people put their ears to the ground to listen. I imitated the cannon and said, 'boom, boom.'" A door on the left-hand of the yard, as we said, leads into the orchard, which is terrible ❧ It is in three parts, we might almost say, in three acts. The first part is a garden, the second the orchard, the third a wood. These three parts have one common enceinte; near the entrance, the buildings of the chateau and the farm, on the left a hedge, on the right a wall, and at the end a wall. The right-hand wall is of brick, the bottom one of stone. You enter the garden first; it slopes, is planted with gooseberry bushes, is covered with wild vegetation, and is

closed by a monumental terrace of cut
stones with balustrades ✒ It was a seig-
neurial garden in the French style, that
preceded Le Notre: now it is ruins and
briars. The pilasters are surmounted by
globes that resemble stone cannon-balls.
Forty-three balustrades are still erect; the
others are lying in the grass, and nearly
all have marks of musket-balls ✒ One
fractured balustrade is laid upon the stem
like a broken leg.
It was in this garden, which is lower than
the orchard, that six voltigeurs of the
First Light Regiment, having got in and
unable to get out, and caught like bears
in a trap, accepted combat with two
Hanoverian companies, one of which
was armed with rifles. The Hanoverians
lined the balustrade and fired down; the
voltigeurs, firing up, six intrepid men
against two hundred, and having no
shelter but the gooseberry bushes, took
a quarter of an hour in dying. You climb
up a few steps and reach the orchard,
properly so called ✒ Here, on these few
square yards, fifteen hundred men fell in
less than an hour. The wall seems ready
to recommence the fight, for the thirty-

eight loop-holes pierced by the English at irregular heights may still be seen. In front of the wall are two English tombs made of granite ❧ There are only loop-holes in the south wall, for the principal attack was on that side ❧ This wall is concealed on the outside by a quickset hedge. The French came up under the impression that they had only to carry this hedge, and found the wall an obstacle and an ambuscade; the English Guards, behind the thirty-eight loop-holes, firing at once a storm of canister and bullets; and Soye's brigade was dashed to pieces against it. Waterloo began thus.

The orchard, however, was taken; as the French had no ladders, they climbed up with their nails. A hand-to-hand fight took place under the trees, and all the grass was soaked with blood, and a battalion of Nassau, seven hundred strong was cut to pieces here ❧ On the outside the wall, against which Kellerman's two batteries were pointed, is pock-marked with cannon-balls ❧ This orchard is sensitive like any other to the month of May; it has its buttercups and its daisies, the grass is tall in it, the plough horses browse in it, hair ropes on which linen is hung to dry occupy the space between the trees, and make the visitor bow his head, and as you walk along your foot sinks in mole holes ✠ In the middle of the grass you notice an uprooted, out-stretched, but still flourishing tree. Major Blackman leant against it to die ✠ Under another large tree close by fell the German General Duplat, a French refugee belonging to a family that fled upon the revocation of the edict of Nantes ✠ Close at hand an old sickly apple tree, poulticed with a bandage of straw and clay, hangs its head. Nearly all the apple trees are dying of old age, and there is not one without its cannon-ball or bullet. Skeletons of dead trees abound in this orchard, ravens fly about in the branches, and at the end is a wood full of violets.

Bauduin killed; Foy wounded; massacre, arson, carnage, a stream composed of English, French, and German blood furiously mingled; a well filled with corpses; the Nassau regiment and the Brunswick regiment destroyed; Duplat killed; Blackman killed; the English Guards mutilated; twenty French battalions of the forty composing Reille's corps decimated; three thousand men in this chateau of Hougomont alone, sabred, gashed, butchered, shot, and burnt,—all this that a peasant may say to a traveler at the present day, "If you like to give me three francs, sir, I will tell you all about the battle of Waterloo."

June 18, 1815

NOW, let us go back, for that is one of the privileges of the narrator, & place ourselves once again in the year 1815. If it had not rained on the night between the 17th and 18th of June, 1815, the future of Europe would have been changed; a few drops of rain more or less made Napoleon oscillate ✺ In order to make Waterloo the end of Austerlitz, Providence only required a little rain, and a cloud crossing the sky at a season when rain was not expected was sufficient to overthrow an empire ✺ The battle of Waterloo could not begin until half-past eleven, and that gave Blucher time to come up ✒ Why? Because the ground was moist and it was necessary for it to become firmer, that the artillery might manœuvre. Napoleon was an artillery officer, & always showed himself one; all his battle plans are made for projectiles. Making artillery converge on a given point was his key to victory. He treated the strategy of the opposing general as a citadel, and breached it; he crushed the weak point under grape-shot, and he began and ended his battles with artillery. Driving in squares, pulverizing regiments, breaking lines, destroying and dispersing masses, all this must be done by striking, striking, striking incessantly, and he confided the task to artillery. It was a formidable method, and, allied to genius, rendered this gloomy pugilist of war invincible for fifteen years.

On June 18, 1815, he counted the more on his artillery, because he held the numerical superiority ✒ Wellington had only one hundred and fifty-nine guns, while Napoleon had two hundred and forty ✒ Had the earth been dry and the artillery able to move, the action would

24

have begun at six o'clock in the morning. It would have been won and over by two in the afternoon, three hours before the Prussian interlude ✒ How much blame was there on Napoleon's side for the loss of this battle? Is the shipwreck imputable to the pilot? Was the evident physical decline of Napoleon at that period complicated by a certain internal diminution? Had twenty years of war worn out the blade as well as the scabbard, the soul as well as the body? Was the veteran being awkwardly displayed in the captain? In a word, was the genius, as many historians of reputation have believed, eclipsed? Was he becoming frenzied, in order to conceal his own weakening from himself? Was he beginning to oscillate and veer with the wind? ✒ Was he becoming unconscious of danger, which is a serious thing in a general? ✒ In that class of great material men who may be called the giants of action, is there an age when genius becomes short-sighted? Old age has no power over ideal genius, with the Dantes and the Michael Angelos old age is growth, but is it declension for the Hannibals and the Bonapartes? ✒ Had

Napoleon lost the direct sense of victory? Had he reached a point where he no longer saw the rock, guessed the snare, and could not discern the crumbling edge of the abyss? Could he not scent catastrophes? ✠ Had the man who formerly knew all the roads to victory and pointed to them with a sovereign finger, from his flashing car, now a mania for leading his tumultuous team of legions to the precipices? ✠ Was he attacked at the age of forty-six by a supreme madness? Was the Titanic charioteer of destiny now only a Phæton?

We do not believe it.

His plan of action, it is allowed by all, was a masterpiece ✠ Go straight at the center of the allied line, make a hole through the enemy, cut him in two, drive the British half over Halle, and the Prussians over Tingres, carry Mont St. Jean, seize Brussels, drive the German into the Rhine and the Englishman into the sea—all this was contained for Napoleon in this battle; afterwards he would see ✠ ✠

We need hardly say that we do not pretend to tell the story of Waterloo here;

one of the generating scenes of the drama
we are recounting is attaching to this battle, but the story of Waterloo has been
already told, and magisterially discussed,
from one point of view by Napoleon,
from another by Charras ❧ For our part
we leave the two historians to contend;
we are only a distant witness, a passer-by
along the plain, a seeker bending over
the earth moulded of human flesh, and
perhaps taking appearances for realities;
we possess neither the military practice
nor the strategic competency that au-
thorizes a system; in our opinion,
a chain of accidents governed
both captains at Waterloo;
& when destiny, that mys-
terious accused, enters
on the scene, we judge
like the people.

The Battlefield

THOSE who wish to form a distinct idea of the battle of Waterloo, need only imagine a capital A laid on the ground. The left leg of the A is the Nivelles road, the right one the Genappe road, while the string of the A is the broken way running from Ohaine to Braine l' Alleud ❧ The top of the A is Mont St. Jean, where Wellington is; the left lower point is Hougomont, were Reille is with Jerome Bonaparte; the right lower point is La Belle Alliance, where Napoleon is ❧ A little below the point where the string of the A meets and cuts the right leg, is La Haye Sainte; & in the center of this string is the exact spot where the battle was concluded. It is here that the lion is placed, the involuntary symbol of the heroism of the old Guard ❧ ❧

The triangle comprised at the top of the A between the two legs & the string, is the plateau of Mont St. Jean; the dispute for this plateau was the whole battle ✒ The wings of the two armies extend to the right and left of the Genappe and Nivelles roads, d'Erlon facing Picton, Reille facing Hill ✒ Behind the point of the A, behind the plateau of St. Jean, is the forest of Soignies ✒ As for the plan itself, imagine a vast undulating ground; each ascent commands the next ascent, and all the undulations ascend to Mont St. Jean, where they form the forest.

Two hostile armies on a battle-field are two wrestlers,—one tries to throw the other; they cling to everything; a thicket is a basis; for want of a village to support it, a regiment gives way; a fall in the plain, a transverse hedge in a good position, a wood, a ravine may arrest the heel of that column which is called an army, and prevent it slipping ✒ The one who leaves the field is beaten; and hence the necessity for the responsible chief to examine the smallest clump of trees, and investigate the slightest rise in the ground. The two generals had attentively studied the plain of Mont St. Jean, which is called at the present day the field of Waterloo. In the previous year, Wellington, with prescient sagacity, had examined it as suitable for a great battle. On this ground and for this duel of June 18, Wellington had the good side and Napoleon the bad; for the English army was above, and the French army below.

It is almost superfluous to sketch here the appearance of Napoleon, mounted and with his telescope in his hand, as he appeared on the heights of Rossomme at the dawn of June 18 ❧ Before we show him, all the world has seen him. The calm profile under the little hat of the Brienne school, the green uniform, the white facings concealing the decorations, the great coat concealing the epaulettes, the red ribbon under the waistcoat, the leather breeches, the white horse with its housings of a purple velvet, having in the corners crowned N's and eagles, riding boots drawn over silk stockings, the silver spurs, the sword of Marengo,—the whole appearance of the last of the Cæsars rises before every mind, applauded by some, and regarded sternly by others ❧ This figure has for a long time stood out all light; this was due to a certain legendary obscuration which most heroes evolve,

and which always conceals the truth for
a longer or shorter period, but at the
present day we have history and light.
That brilliancy called history is pitiless;
it has this strange and divine thing about
it, that, all light as it is, and because it is
light, it often throws shadows over spots
before luminous, it makes of the same
man two different phantoms, and one attacks the other, and the darkness of the
despot struggles with the lustre of the
captain. Hence comes a truer proportion
in the definite appreciation of nations;
Babylon violated, diminishes Alexander; Rome enchained, diminishes
Cæsar; Jerusalem killed, diminishes Titus. Tyranny follows
the tyrant, & it is a misfortune
for a man to leave behind
him a night which
has his form.

The Battle

LL the world knows the first phase of this battle; a troubled, uncertain, hesitating opening, dangerous for both armies, more so for the English than the French ✴ It had rained all night; the ground was saturated; the rain had collected in hollows of the plain as in tubs; at certain points the ammunition wagons had sunk in up to the axletrees and the girths of the horses; if the wheat and barley laid low by this mass of moving vehicles had not filled the ruts, and made a litter under the wheels, any movement, especially in the valleys, in the direction of Papelotte, would have been impossible. The battle began late, for Napoleon, as we have explained, was accustomed to hold all his artillery in hand like a pistol, aiming first at one point, then at another of the battle, and he resolved to wait until the field batteries could gallop freely and for this purpose it was necessary that the sun

should appear and dry the ground ﺑ But the sun did not come out; it was no longer the rendezvous of Austerlitz ﺑ When the first cannon-shot was fired, the English General Colville drew out his watch, and saw that it was twenty-five minutes to twelve.

The action was commenced furiously, more so perhaps than the emperor desired, by the French left wing on Hougomont. At the same time Napoleon attacked the center by hurling Quiot's brigade on La Haye Sainte, and Ney pushed the French right wing against the English left, which was leaning upon Papelotte. The attack on Hougomont was, to a certain extent, a feint, for the plan was to attract Wellington there, and make him strengthen his left. This plan would have succeeded had not the four companies of Guards and Perponcher's Belgian division firmly held the position, and Wellington, instead of massing his troops, found it only necessary to send as a reinforcement four more companies of Guards and a battalion of Brunswickers ﺑ The attack of the French right on Papelotte was serious; to destroy the English left, cut the Brussels

road, bar the passage for any possible
Prussians, force Mont St. Jean, drive
back Wellington on Hougomont, then on
Braine l' Alleud, and then on Halle, —
nothing was more distinct. Had not a few
incidents supervened, this attack would
have succeeded, for Papelotte was taken
and La Haye Sainte carried.

There is a detail to be noticed here ❧ In
the English infantry, especially in Kempt's
brigade, there were many recruits, and
these young soldiers valiantly withstood
our formidable foot, and they behaved
excellently as sharpshooters. The soldier
when thrown out, being left to some extent to his own resources, becomes as it
were his own general; and these recruits
displayed something of the French inven-
tion and fury. These novices displayed
an impulse, and it displeased Wellington.
❡ After the taking of La Haye Sainte, the
battle vacillated ❧ There is an obscure
interval in this day, between twelve and
four; the middle of this battle is almost
indistinct, and participates in the gloom
of the melee. A twilight sets in, and we
perceive vast fluctuations in this mist, a
dizzying mirage, the panoply of war at

that day, unknown in our times; flaming colpacks; flying sabretasches; cross-belts; Grenadier bearskins; Hussar dolmans; red boots with a thousand wrinkles; heavy shakos enwreathed with gold twist; the nearly black Brunswick infantry mingled with the scarlet infantry of England; the English soldiers wearing clumsy round white cushions for epaulettes; the Hanoverian light horse with their leathern helmets, brass bands, and red horsetails; the Highlanders with their bare knees and checkered plaids, and the long white gaiters of our Grenadiers, — pictures, but not strategic lines; what a Salvator Rosa, but not a Gribeauval, would have revelled in ❧ ❧ ❧

A certain amount of tempest is always mingled with a battle ❧ Every historian traces to some extent the lineament that pleases him in the hurly-burly. Whatever the combination of the generals may be, the collision of armed masses has incalculable ebbs and flows; in action the two plans of the leaders enter into each other and destroy their shape ❧ The line of battle floats and winds like a thread, the streams of blood flow illogically, the

fronts of armies undulate, the regiments
in advancing or retiring form capes or
gulfs, and all these rocks are continually
shifting their position; where infantry
was, artillery arrives; where artillery was,
cavalry dash in; the battalions are smoke.
There was something there, but when
you look for it it has disappeared; the
gloomy masses advance and retreat; a
species of breath from the tomb impels,
drives back, swells, and disperses these
tragic multitudes ✺ What is a battle? An
oscillation. The immobility of a mathe-
matical plan expresses a minute and not
a day. To paint a battle, those powerful
painters who have chaos in their pencils
are needed ✺ Rembrandt is worth more
than Vandermeulin, for Vandermeulin,
exact at midday, is incorrect at three
o'clock. Geometry is deceived, and the
hurricane alone is true, and it is this that
gives Folard the right to contradict Polyb-
ius. Let us add that there is always a certain
moment in which the battle degenerates
into a combat, is particularized & broken
up into countless detail facts which, to
borrow the expression of Napoleon himself, "Belong rather to the biography of

regiments than to the history of the army."
‣ The historian, in such a case, has the evident right to sum up, he can only catch the principal outlines of the struggle, and it is not given to any narrator, however conscientious he may be, to absolutely fix the form of that horrible cloud which is called a battle.

This, which is true of all great armed collisions, is also peculiarly applicable to Waterloo; still, at a certain moment in the afternoon, the battle began to assume a settled shape.

In The Afternoon

AT about four o'clock in the afternoon, the situation of the English army was serious. The Prince of Orange commanded the center, Hill the right, and Picton the left. The Prince of Orange, wild and intrepid, shouted to the Dutch Belgians: ‣ "Nassau Brunswick, never yield an inch." Hill, fearfully weakened, had just fallen back on Wellington, while Picton was dead. At the very moment when the English took from the French the flag of the One Hundred-fifth Line Regiment, the French killed General Picton with a bullet through his head. The battle had two bases for Wellington, Hougomont and La Haye Sainte. Hougomont still held out, though on fire, while La Haye Sainte was lost ↦ Of the German battalion that defended it, forty-two men only survived; all the officers but five were killed or taken prisoners. Three thousand combatants had been massacred in that focus; a sergeant of the English Guards, the first boxer of England & reputed invulnerable by his comrades, had been killed there by a little French drummer ↦ Barny was dislodged, and Alten was sabred; several flags had been lost, one belonging to Alten's division and one to the Luxembourg battalion, which was borne by a prince of the Deux-ponts family ↦ The Scotch Greys no longer existed; Ponsonby's heavy dragoons were cut to pieces, —this brave cavalry had given away before the Lancers of Bex and the Cuirassiers of Traver ↦ Of twelve hundred sabres only six hundred remained; of three lieutenant-colonels, two were kissing the ground, Hamilton wounded, and Mather killed ❧ Ponsonby had fallen, pierced by seven lance wounds; Gordon was dead, March was dead, and two divisions, the fifth and sixth, were destroyed. Hougomont attacked ❧ La Haye Sainte taken; there was only one knot left, the center, which still held out. Wellington reinforced it; he called in Hill from Merbe-Braine and Chasse from Braine l' Alleud. ⁌ The center of the English army, which was slightly concave, very dense and compact, was strongly situated; it occupied the plateau of Mont St. Jean, having the village behind it, and before it the slope, which at that time was rather steep. ❧ It was supported by that strong stone house, which at that period was a domainial property of Nivelles, standing at the cross-road, and an edifice dating from the sixteenth century, so robust that the cannon-balls rebounded without doing it any injury ❧ All round the plateau the English had cut through the hedges at certain spots, formed embrasures in the hawthorns, thrust guns between branches and loopholed the shrubs,—their artillery was ambuscaded under the brambles ∙ This Punic task, incontestably authorized by the rules of war which permit snares, had been so well effected that Haxo, who had been sent by the emperor at eight o'clock to reconnoiter the enemy's batteries, returned to tell Napoleon that there was no obstacle, with the exception of the barricades blocking the Nivelles and Genappe roads ∙ It was the season when the wheat is still standing, & along the edge of the plateau a battalion of Kempt's brigade, the Ninety-fifth, was lying in the tall corn. Thus assured and supported, the center of the Anglo-Dutch army was in a good position.

The peril of this position was the forest of Soignies, at that time contiguous to the battle-field and intersected by the ponds of Groenendael and Boitsford. An army could not have fallen back into it without being dissolved, regiments would have been broken up at once, and the artillery lost in the marshes. The retreat, according to the opinion of several professional men, contradicted, it is true, by others, would have been a flight ∙ Wellington added to this center a brigade of Chasse's removed from the right wing, one of Wicke's from the left wing, and Clinton's division ✒ He gave his English — Halkett's regiments, Mitchell's brigade, and Maitland's guards — as epaulments and counterforts, the Brunswick infantry, the Nassau contingent, Kielmansegge's Hanoverians, and Ompteda's Germans ✒ He had thus twenty-six battalions under his hand; as Charras says, 'The right wing deployed behind the center.' An enormous battery was masked by earth bags, at the very spot where what is called "The Museum of Waterloo" now stands, and Wellington also had in a little hollow Somerset's Dragoon Guards, counting one thousand four hundred sabres. They were the other moiety of the so justly celebrated English cavalry; though Ponsonby was destroyed, Somerset remained. The battery which, had it been completed, would have been almost a redoubt, was arranged behind a very low wall, hastily lined with sand bags and a wide slope of earth ✒ This work was not finished, as there was not time to pallisade it.

Wellington, restless but impassive, was

mounted, and remained for the whole
day in the same attitude, a little in front
of the old mill of Mont St. Jean, which
still exists, and under an elm-tree, which
an Englishman, an enthusiastical Vandal,
afterwards bought for two hundred francs,
cut down and carried away. Wellington
was coldly heroic; there was a shower of
cannon-balls, and his aid-de-camp Gordon
was killed by his side. Lord Hill, pointing
to a bursting shell, said to him, "My
Lord, what are your instructions, and
what orders do you leave us, if you are
killed?" "Do as I am doing," Wellington
answered ❧ To Clinton he said, laconic-
ally, "Hold out here to the last man."
The day was evidently turning badly,
and Wellington cried to his old comrades
of Vittoria, Talavera, and Salamanca,
"Boys, can you think of giving way?
Remember old England."
About four o'clock, the English line fell
back all at once; nothing was visible on
the crest of the plateau but artillery and
sharpshooters, the rest had disappeared.
The regiments, expelled by the French
shell and cannon-balls, fell back into the
hollow, which at the present day is in-

tersected by the lane that runs to the farm of Mont St. Jean ᔓ A retrograde movement began, the English front withdrew. Wellington was recoiling. "It is the beginning of the retreat," Napoleon cried.

Napoleon in Good Humor

HE emperor, though ill and suffering on horseback from a local injury, had never been so goodtempered as on this day. ᔓ From the morning his impenetrability had been smiling, and on June 18, 1815, this profound soul, coated with granite, was radiant. The man who had been sombre at Austerlitz was gay at Waterloo ᔓ The greatest predestined men offer these contradictions, for our joys are a shadow and the supreme smile belongs to God. ᔓ *Ridet Cæsar, Pompeius flebit*, the legionaries of the Fulminatrix legion used to say. On this occasion Pompey was not destined to weep, but it is certain that Cæsar laughed ᔓ At one o'clock in the

morning, amid the rain and storm, he had
explored with Bertrand the hills near
Rossomme, and was pleased to see the
long lines of English fires illumining the
horizon from Frischemont to Braine l'Alleud. It seemed to him as if destiny had
made an appointment with him on a fixed
day and was punctual ᴈ⊷ He stopped his
horse, & remained for some time motionless, looking at the lightning and listening
to the thunder. The fatalist was heard to
cast into the night the mysterious words,
—"We are agreed." Napoleon was mis-
taken, they were no longer agreed.
He had not slept for a moment; all the
instants of the past night had been marked
with joy for him ᴈ⊷ He rode through the
entire line of main guards, stopping every
now and then to speak to the videttes.
At half-past two he heard the sound of a
marching column near Hougomont, and
believed for a moment in a retreat on the
side of Wellington. He said to Bertrand,
—"The English rear-guard is preparing
to decamp. I shall take prisoners the six
thousand English who have just landed
at Ostende." He talked cheerfully, & had
regained the spirits he had displayed dur-

ing the landing of March 1st, when he showed the grand marshal the enthusiastic peasant of the Juan Gulf and said,— "Well, Bertrand, here is a reinforcement already." On the night between June 17 and 18 he made fun of Wellington: "This little Englishman requires a lesson," said Napoleon ∾ The rain became twice as violent, and it thundered while the emperor was speaking. At half-past three in the morning, he lost one illusion; officers sent to reconnoiter informed him that the enemy was making no movement. Nothing was stirring, not a single bivouac fire was extinguished, and the English army was sleeping. The silence was profound on earth, and there was only noise in the heavens ∾ At four o'clock a peasant was brought to him by the scouts; this peasant had served as guide to a brigade of English cavalry, probably Vivian's, which had taken up a position on the extreme left in the village of Ohain. At five o'clock two Belgian deserters informed him that they had just left their regiments, and the English army meant fighting ∾ "All the better," cried Napoleon, "I would sooner crush them than drive them back."

At daybreak he dismounted on the slope
which forms the angle of the Plancenoit
road, had a kitchen table & a peasant chair
brought from the farm of Rossomme, sat
down with a truss of straw for a carpet,
and laid on the table the map of the battle-
field, saying to Soult,—"It is a pretty
chess-board." Owing to the night rain,
the commissariat wagons, which stuck in
the muddy roads, did not arrive by daybreak ❧ The troops had not slept, were
wet through and fasting, but this did not
prevent Napoleon from exclaiming cheerfully to Soult,—"We have ninety chances
out of a hundred in our favor." ❧ At
eight o'clock the emperor's breakfast was
brought, and he invited several generals
to share it with him. While breakfasting
somebody said that Wellington had been
the last evening but one at a ball in Brussels, and Soult, the rough soldier with his
archbishop's face, remarked, "The ball
will be to-day." The emperor teased Ney
for saying,—"Wellington will not be so
simple as to wait for your majesty." This
was his usual manner ❧ "He was fond
of a joke," says Fleury de Chaboulon;
"The basis of his character was a pleasant

46

humor," says Gourgaud; "He abounded with jests, more peculiar than witty," says Benjamin Constant. This gaiety of the giant is worth dwelling on; it was he who called his Grenadiers, "Growlers;" he pinched their ears and pulled their mustaches." "The emperor was always playing tricks with us," was a remark made by one of them. During the mysterious passage from Elba to France, on February 27, the French brig of war, the Zephyr, met the Inconstant, on board which Napoleon was concealed, and inquiring after Napoleon, the emperor, who still had in his hat the white and violet cockade studded with bees which he had adopted at Elba, himself laughingly took up the speaking trumpet, and answered, —"The emperor is quite well." A man who jests in this way is on familiar terms with events. Napoleon had several outbursts of this laughter during the breakfast of Waterloo; after breakfast he reflected for a quarter of an hour; then two generals sat down on the truss of straw with a pen in their hand, and a sheet of paper on their knee, and the emperor dictated to them the plan of the battle ❧ At nine

o'clock, the moment when the French
army, echelonned and moving in five
columns, began to deploy, the divisions in
two lines, the artillery between, the bands
in front, drums rattling & bugles braying
—a powerful, mighty, joyous army, a sea
of bayonets and helmets on the horizon,
the emperor, much affected, twice exclaimed, — "Magnificent! magnificent!"
❦ Between nine & half-past ten, although
it seems incredible, the whole army took
up position, & was drawn up in six lines,
forming, to repeat the emperor's expression, "The figure of six V's." ✺ A few
minutes after the formation of the line,
and in the midst of that profound silence
which precedes the storm of a battle, the
emperor, seeing three twelve-pounder batteries defile, which had been detached by
his orders from Erlon, Reille, & Lobau's
brigades, and which were intended to
begin the action at the spot where the
Nivelles & Genappe roads crossed, tapped
Haxo on the shoulder, and said, "There
are twenty-four pretty girls, general." ✺
Sure of the result, he encouraged with a
smile the company of sappers of the first
corps as it passed him, which he had se-

lected to barricade itself in Mont St. Jean, so soon as the village was carried. All this security was only crossed by one word of human pity; on seeing at his left, at the spot where there is now a large tomb, the admirable Scotch Greys massed with their superb horses, he said, "It is a pity." Then he mounted his horse, rode toward Rossomme, & selected as his observatory a narrow strip of grass on the right of the road running from Genappe to Brussels, and this was his second station. The third station, the one he took at seven in the evening, is formidable, — it is a rather lofty mound which still exists, & behind which the guard was massed in a hollow. Around this mound, the balls ricochetted on the pavement of the road and reached Napoleon ❧ As at Brienne, he had round his head the whistle of bullets & canister. Almost at the spot where his horse's hoofs stood, cannon-balls, old sabre-blades, and shapeless rust-eaten projectiles, have been picked up; a few years ago, a live shell was dug up, the fusee of which had broken off. It was at this station that the emperor said to his guide, Lacoste, a hostile timid peasant, who was fastened to a hussar's

saddle, & tried at each volley of canister
to hide himself behind Napoleon, " You
ass, it is shameful; you will be killed in
the back " ๛ The person who is writing
these lines himself found, while digging
up the sand in the friable slope of this
mound, the remains of a shell rotted by
the oxide of forty-six years, and pieces of
iron which broke like sticks of barley-
sugar between his fingers.
Everybody is aware that the undulations
of the plains on which the encounter
between Napoleon and Wellington took
place, are no longer as they were on June
18, 1815 ๛ On taking from this mournful
plain the material to make a monument,
it was deprived of its real relics, & history,
disconcerted, no longer recognizes itself;
in order to glorify, they disfigured. Wellington, on seeing Waterloo two years
after, exclaimed, "My battle-field has been
altered." ๛ Where the huge pyramid of
earth surmounted by a lion now stands,
there was a crest which on the side of the
Nivelles road had a practicable ascent,
but which on the side of the Genappe
road was almost an escarpment ๛ The
elevation of this escarpment may still be

imagined by the height of the two great
tombs which skirt the road from Genappe
to Brussels; the English tomb on the left,
the German tomb on the right. There is
no French tomb,—for France the whole
plain is a sepulcher. Through the thou-
sands of cart-loads of earth employed in
erecting the mound, which is one hundred and fifty feet high and half a mile in
circumference, the plateau of Mont St.
Jean is now accessible by a gentle incline,
but on the day of the battle, & especially
on the side of La Haye Sainte, it was
steep & abrupt. The incline was so sharp
that the English gunners could not see
beneath them the farm situated in the
bottom of the valley, which was the center of the fight ✎ On June 18, 1815, the
rain had rendered the steep road more
difficult, and the troops not only had to
climb up but slipped in the mud. Along
the center of the crest of the plateau ran a
species of ditch, which it was impossible
for a distant observer to guess ✎ We will
state what this ditch was. Braine l'Alleud
is a Belgian village and Ohain is another;
these villages, both concealed in hollows,
are connected by a road about a league

and a half in length, which traverses an undulating plain, and frequently buries itself between hills, so as to become at certain spots a ravine. In 1815, as to-day, this road crossed the crest of the plateau of Mont St. Jean; but at the present day it is level with the ground, while at that time it was a hollow way ❧ The two slopes have been carried away to form the monumental mound. This road was, and still is, a trench for the greater part of the distance; a hollow trench, in some places twelve feet deep, whose scarped sides were washed down here and there by the winter rains. Accidents occurred there; the road was so narrow where it entered Braine l'Alleud, that a wayfarer was crushed there by a wagon, as is proved by a stone cross standing near the graveyard, which gives the name of the dead man as "Monsieur Bernard Debruc, trader, of Brussels," & the date, "February, 1637." It was so deep on the plateau of Mont St. Jean, that a peasant, one Mathieu Nicaise, was crushed there in 1783 by a fall of earth, as is proved by another stone cross, the top of which disappeared in the excavations, but whose overthrown pedestal

is still visible on the grass slope to the left
of the road between La Haye Sainte and
the farm of Mont St. Jean. On the day of
the battle, this hollow way, whose exist-
ence nothing revealed, a trench on the
top of the escarpment, a rut hidden in the
earth, was invisible, that is to say, terrible.

Emperor Asks a Question

NAPOLEON, was cheer-
ful on the morning of
Waterloo, & had reason
to be so, for the plan he
had drawn up was admi-
rable ℘ Once the battle
had begun, its various
incidents; the resistance
of Hougomont; the te-
nacity of La Haye Sainte; Bauduin killed,
Foy placed *hors de combat;* the unexpected wall against which Soye's brigade
was broken; the fatal rashness of Guilleminot, who had no petards or powder-bags to
destroy the farm gates; the sticking of
the artillery in the mud; the fifteen guns
without escort captured by Uxbridge in a
hollow way; the slight effect of the shells

falling in the English lines, which buried themselves in the moistened ground, and only produced a volcano of dirt, so that the troops were merely plastered with mud; the inutility of Piret's demonstration on Braine l'Alleud, and the whole of his cavalry, fifteen squadrons, almost annihilated; the English right but slightly disquieted and the left poorly attacked; Ney's strange mistake in massing instead of echelonning the four divisions of the first corps; a depth of twenty-seven ranks and a line of two hundred men given up in this way to the canister; the frightful gaps made by the cannon-balls in these masses; the attacking columns disunited; the oblique battery suddenly unmasked on their flank; Bourgeois, Donzelot, and Durutte in danger; Quiot repulsed; Lieutenant Viot, that Hercules who came from the polytechnic school, wounded at the moment when he was beating in with an axe the gates of La Haye Sainte, under the plunging fire of the English barricade on the Genappe road; Marcognet's division caught between infantry & cavalry, shot down from the wheat by Best and Pack, and sabered by Ponsonby; its battery of

seven guns spiked; the Prince of Saxe
Weimar holding & keeping in defiance of
Count d'Erlon, Frischemont of Smohain;
the flags of the One Hundred and Fifth &
Forty-fifth regiments which he had captured; the Prussian black Hussar stopped
by the scouts of the flying column of
three hundred chasseurs, who were beating the country between Wavre and
Plancenoit; the alarming things which
this man said; Grouchy's delay; the fifteen hundred men killed in less than
an hour in the orchard of Hougomont;
the eighteen hundred laid low even in
a shorter space of time round La Haye
Sainte;—all these stormy incidents, pass-
ing like battle-clouds before Napoleon,
had scarce disturbed his glance or cast a
gloom over this imperial face, Napoleon
was accustomed to look steadily at war; he
never reckoned up the poignant details;
he cared little for figures, provided that
they gave the total—victory. If the commencement went wrong, he did not alarm
himself, as he believed himself master and
owner of the end; he knew how to wait,
and treated destiny as an equal. He seemed
to say to fate, "You would not dare!"

⸤ One half light, one half shade, Napoleon felt himself protected in good & tolerated in evil ᴒ There was, or he fancied there was, for him a connivance, we might say, almost a complicity, on the part of events, equivalent to the ancient invulnerability; and yet, when a man has behind him the Beresina, Leipzig, and Fontainebleau, it seems as if he could defy Waterloo ᴒ A mysterious frown becomes visible on the face of heaven ᴒ At the moment when Wellington retrograded, Napoleon quivered ᴒ He suddenly saw the plateau of Mont St. Jean deserted, and the front of the English army disappear. The emperor half-raised himself in his stirrups, and the flash of victory passed into his eyes. If Wellington were driven back into the forest of Soignies and destroyed, it would be the definitive overthrow of England by France. It would be Cressy, Poictiers, Malplaquet, & Ramilies avenged, the man of Marengo would erase Agincourt ᴒ The emperor, while meditating on this tremendous result, turned his telescope to all parts of the battle-field. His Guards, standing at ease behind him, gazed at him with a sort of religious awe ᴒ He was reflecting, he examined the slopes, noted the inclines, scrutinized the clumps of trees, the patches of barley, and the paths; he seemed to be counting every tuft of gorse. He looked with some fixity at the English barricades, two large masses of felled trees, the one on the Genappe road defended by two guns, the only ones of all the English artillery which commanded the battle-field, & the one on the Nivelles road, behind which flashed the Dutch bayonets of Chasse's brigade. He remarked near this barricade the old chapel of St. Nicholas, which is at the corner of the cross-road leading to Braine l'Alleud ॐ He bent down and spoke in a low voice to the guide Lacoste ॐ The guide shook his head with a probably perfidious negative ॐ ॐ

The emperor drew himself up and reflected; Wellington was retiring, and all that was needed now was to complete this retreat by an overthrow. Napoleon hurriedly turned and sent off a messenger at full speed to Paris to announce that the battle was gained. Napoleon was one of those geniuses from whom thunder issues, and he had just found his thunder-stroke;

he gave Milhaud's Cuirassiers orders to carry the plateau of Mont St. Jean ❧ ❧

A Surprise

THEY were three thousand five hundred in number, and formed a front a quarter of a league in length; they were gigantic men mounted on colossal horses ❧ They formed twenty-six squadrons, and had behind them, as a support, Lefebvre Desnouette's division, composed of the one hundred & sixty gendarmes, the chasseurs of the Guard, eleven hundred and ninety-seven sabres, & the lancers of the Guard, eight hundred and eighty lances ❧ They wore a helmet without a plume, and a cuirass of wrought steel, and were armed with pistols and a straight sabre. In the morning the whole army had admired them when they came up at nine o'clock, with bugles sounding, while all the bands played "Veillons au salut de l'Empire," in close column with one battery on their flank, the others in their center, and deployed in two ranks, and took their place in that powerful second line, so skilfully formed by Napoleon, which, having at its extreme left Kellermann's Cuirassiers, and on its extreme right Milhaud's Cuirassiers, seemed to be endowed with two wings of steel.

The aid-de-camp Bernard carried to them the emperor's order; Ney drew his sabre and placed himself at their head, and the mighty squadrons started. Then a formidable spectacle was seen; the whole of this cavalry, with raised sabres, with standards flying, and formed in columns of division, descended, with one movement and as one man, with the precision of a bronze battering-ram opening a breach, the hill of the Belle Alliance ❧ They entered the formidable valley in which so many men had already fallen, disappeared in the smoke, & then, emerging from the gloom, reappeared on the other side of the valley, still in a close compact column, mounting at a trot, under a tremendous canister fire, the frightful muddy incline of the plateau of Mont St. Jean. They ascended it, stern, threatening, and imperturbable; between the breaks in the artillery and musketry fire, the colossal tramp could be heard ❧ As they formed two divisions, they were in two columns; Wathier's division was on the right, Delord's on the left ❧ At a distance it appeared as if two immense steel lizards were crawling toward the crest of the plateau; they traversed the battle-field like a flash.

Nothing like it had been seen since the capture of the great redoubt of the Moskova by the heavy cavalry; Murat was missing, but Ney was there. It seemed as if this mass had become a monster, and had but one soul; each squadron undulated, and swelled like the rings of a polyp ❧ This could be seen through a vast smoke which was rent asunder at intervals; it was a pell-mell of helmets, shouts, and sabres, a stormy bounding of horses among cannon, and a disciplined and terrible array; while above it all flashed the cuirasses like the scales of the dragon. Such narratives seemed to belong to another age; something like this vision was doubtless traceable in the old Orphean epics describing the men-horses, the ancient hippanthropists, those Titans with human faces and equestrian chest whose gallop escaladed Olympus, — horrible, sublime, invulnerable beings, gods & brutes. It was a curious numerical coincidence that twenty-six battalions were preparing to receive the charge of these twenty-six squadrons ❧ Behind the crest of the plateau, in the shadow of the masked battery, thirteen English squares, each of two battalions and formed two deep, with seven men in the first lines and six in the second, were waiting, calm, dumb, & motionless, with their muskets, for what was coming ❧ They did not see the cuirassiers, and the cuirassiers did not see them; they merely heard this tide of men ascending. They heard the swelling sound of three thousand horses, the alternating and symmetrical sound of the hoof, the clang of the cuirasses, the clash of the sabres, and a species of great and formidable breathing. ❧ There was a long and terrible silence, and then a long file of raised arms, brandishing sabres, and helmets, and bugles & standards, and three thousand heads with great mustaches, shouting "Long live the emperor!" appeared above the crest. The whole of this cavalry debouched on the plateau, & it was like the commencement of an earthquake.

All at once, terrible to relate, the head of the column of cuirassiers facing the English left reared with a fearful clamor ❧ On reaching the culminating point of the crest, furious and eager to make their exterminating dash on the English squares and guns, the cuirassiers noticed between them and the English a trench, a grave. It was the hollow road of Ohain. It was a frightful moment,—the ravine was there, unexpected, yawning, almost precipitous, beneath the horses' feet, and with a depth of twelve feet between its two sides. The second rank thrust the first into the abyss; the horses reared, fell back, slipped with all four feet in the air, crushing & throwing their riders. There was no means of escaping; the entire column was one huge projectile ❧ The force acquired to crush the English, crushed the French, and the inexorable ravine would not yield till it was filled up. Men & horses rolled into it pell-mell, crushing each other, & making one large charnel-house of the gulf, and when this grave was full of living men the rest passed over them ❧ Nearly one-third of Dubois' brigade rolled into this abyss ❧ This commenced the loss of the battle. A local tradition, which evidently exaggerates, says that two thousand horses and fifteen hundred men were buried in the hollow way of Ohain. These figures probably comprise the other corpses cast into the ravine on the day after the battle. Napoleon, before ordering this charge, had surveyed the ground, but had been unable to see this hollow way, which did not form even a ripple on the crest of the plateau. Warned, however, by the little white chapel which marks its juncture with the Nivelles road, he had asked Lacoste a question, probably as to whether there was any obstacle ❧ The guide answered no, and we might almost say that Napoleon's catastrophe was brought about by a peasant's shake of the head.

¶ Other fatalities were yet to arise. Was it possible for Napoleon to win the battle? ❧ We answer in the negative ❧ Why? On account of Wellington, on account of Blucher? ❧ No; on account of God ❧ Bonaparte, victor at Waterloo, did not harmonize with the law of the nineteenth century. Another series of facts was preparing, in which Napoleon had no longer a place; the ill will of events had been displayed long previously ❧ It was time for this vast man to fall; his excessive weight in human destiny disturbed the balance. This individual alone was of more account than the universal group; such plethoras of human vitality concentrated in a single head—the world, mounting to one man's brain—would be mortal to civilization if they endured ❧ The moment had arrived for the incorruptible supreme equity to reflect, and it is probable that the principles and elements on which the regular gravitations of the moral order as of the material order depend, complained. ❧ Streaming blood, over-crowded graveyards, mothers in tears, are formidable pleaders ❧ When the earth is suffering from an excessive burden, there are mysterious groans from the shadow, which the abyss hears. Napoleon had been denounced in infinitude, and his fall was decided. ❧ Waterloo is not a battle, but a transformation of the universe ❧ ❧

The Plateau of Mont St. Jean

THE battery was unmasked simultaneously with the ravine,—sixty guns and the thirteen squares thundered at the cuirassiers at pointblank range ❧ The intrepid General Delord gave a military salute to the English battery ❧ The whole of the English field artillery had entered the squares at a gallop; the cuirassiers had not even a moment for reflection. The disaster of the hollow way had decimated but not discouraged them, they were of that nature of men whose hearts grow large when their number is diminished. Wathier's column alone suffered in the disaster; but Delord's column, which he had ordered to wheel to the left, as if he suspected the trap, arrived entire. The cuirassiers rushed at the English squares at full gallop, with hanging bridles, sabres in their mouths, & pistols in their hands. There are moments in a battle when the soul hardens a man, so that it changes the soldier into a statue, and all flesh becomes granite ❧ The English battalions, though fiercely assailed, did not move. Then there was a frightful scene, all the faces of the English squares were attacked simultaneously, and a frenzied whirl surrounded them. But the cold infantry remained impassive; the front rank kneeling received the cuirassiers on their bayonets, while the second fired at them; behind the second rank the artillerymen loaded their guns, the front of the square opened to let an eruption of canister pass, and then closed again. The cuirassiers responded by attempts to crush their foe; their great horses reared, leaped over the bayonets, & landed in the center of the four living walls. The cannon-balls made gaps in the cuirassiers, and the cuirassiers made breaches in the squares ❧ Files of men disappeared, trampled down by the horses, and bayonets were buried in the entrails of these centaurs ❧ Hence arose horrible wounds, such as were probably never seen elsewhere. The squares, were broken by the impetuous cavalry, contracted without yielding an inch of ground; inexhaustible in canister they produced an explosion in the midst of the

assailants. The aspect of this combat was monstrous; the squares were no longer battalions, but craters; these cuirassiers were no longer cavalry, but a tempest,— each square was a volcano attacked by a storm; the lava combated the lightning.
❡ The extreme right square, the most exposed of all, as it was in the air, was nearly annihilated in the first attack. It was formed of the Seventy-fifth Highlanders; the piper in the center, while his comrades were being exterminated around him, was seated on a drum, with his pibroch under his arm, and playing mountain airs. These Scotchmen died, thinking of Ben Lothian, as the Greeks did, remembering Argos ✺ A cuirassier's sabre, by cutting through the pibroch & the arm that held it, stopped the tune by killing the player.
The cuirassiers, relatively few in number, and reduced by the catastrophe of the ravine, had against them nearly the whole English army; but they multiplied them- selves, and each man was worth ten ✺ Some Hanoverian battalions, however, gave way; Wellington saw it and thought of his cavalry ✺ Had Napoleon at this moment thought of his infantry, the battle

would have been won, and this forgetful-
ness was his great and fatal fault ❧ All at
once the assailers found themselves assailed; the English cavalry were on their
backs, before them the squares, behind
them Somerset with the one thousand four
hundred dragoon guards ❧ Somerset had
on his right Dornberg with the German
chevau-legers, and on his left Trip with
the Belgian carbineers; the cuirassiers, attacked on the flank and in front, before
and behind, by infantry and cavalry, were
compelled to make a front on all sides.
But what did they care? ❧ They were a
whirlwind, their bravery became indescribable ❧ ❧
In addition, they had behind them the
still thundering battery, and it was only
in such a way that these men could be
wounded in the back ❧ One of these
cuirasses with a hole through the left
scapula, is in the Waterloo Museum. For
such Frenchmen, nothing less than such
Englishmen was required ❧ It was no
longer a melee, it was a headlong fury, a
hurricane of flashing swords. In an instant
the one thousand four hundred dragoons
were only eight hundred; & Fuller, their

lieutenant-colonel, was dead. Ney dashed up with Lefebvre Desnouette's Lancers and Chasseurs; the plateau of Mont St. Jean was taken and retaken, and taken again. The cuirassiers left the cavalry to attack the infantry, or to speak more correctly, all these men collared each other and did not loose their hold. The squares still held out after twelve assaults. Ney had four horses killed under him, and one-half of the cuirassiers remained on the plateau. This struggle lasted two hours. The English army was profoundly shaken; & there is no doubt that, had not the cuirassiers been weakened in their attack by the disaster of the hollow way, they would have broken through the center & decided the victory. This extraordinary cavalry petrified Clinton, who had seen Talavera and Badajoz ᔆ Wellington, three parts vanquished, admired heroically; he said in a low voice, "Splendid!" The cuirassiers annihilated seven squares out of thirteen, captured or spiked sixty guns, and took six English regimental flags, which three cuirassiers & three chasseurs of the guard carried to the emperor before the farm of La Belle Alliance.

Wellington's situation had grown worse. ⋙ This strange battle resembled a fight between two savage wounded men, who constantly lose their blood while continuing the struggle ⋙ Which would be the first to fall? The combat for the plateau continued ⋙ How far did the cuirassiers get? No one could say; but it is certain that on the day after the battle, a cuirassier and his horse were found dead on the weighing machine of Mont St. Jean, at the very spot where the Nivelles, Genappe, La Hulpe, & Brussels roads intersect each other ⋙ This horseman had pierced the English lines. One of the men who picked up this corpse still lives at Mont St. Jean; his name is Dehaye, and he was eighteen years of age at the time ⋙ Wellington felt himself giving way, and the crisis was close at hand ⋙ The cuirassiers had not succeeded, in the sense that the English center had not been broken. Everybody held the plateau, and nobody held it; but in the end, the greater portion remained in the hands of the English ⋙ Wellington had the village and the plain; Ney, only the crest and the slope. Both sides seemed to have taken root in this mournful soil.

70

But the weakness of the English seemed irremediable, for the hemorrhage of this army was horrible ❧ Kempt on the left wing asked for reinforcements. "There are none," Wellington replied ❧ Almost at the same moment, by a strange coincidence which depicts the exhaustion of both armies, Ney asked Napoleon for infantry, & Napoleon answered, "Infantry? Where does he expect me to get them? Does he think I can make them?"
Still the English army was the worse of the two, the furious attacks of these great squadrons with their iron cuirasses and steel chests had crushed their infantry. A few men round the colors marked the place of a regiment, and some battalions were only commanded by a captain or a lieutenant ❧ Alten's division, already so maltreated at La Haye Sainte, was nearly destroyed; the intrepid Belgians of Van Kluze's brigade lay among the wheat along the Nivelles road; hardly any were left of those Dutch Grenadiers who, in 1811, fought Wellington in Spain, on the French side, and who, in 1815, joined the English and fought Napoleon. The loss in officers was considerable; Lord Uxbridge, who

had his leg interred the next day, had a fractured knee ❧ If on the side of the French in this contest of the cuirassiers, Delord, l'Heretier, Colbert, Duof, Travers & Blancard were *hors de combat*, on the side of the English, Alten was wounded, Barnes was wounded, Delancey killed, Van Meeren killed, Ompteda killed, Wellington's staff decimated,—and England had the heaviest scale in this balance of blood ❧ The Second Regiment of footguards had lost five lieutenant-colonels, four captains, and three ensigns; the First Battalion of the Thirtieth had lost twenty-four officers, and one hundred and twelve men; the Seventy-ninth Highlanders had twenty-four officers wounded, & eighteen officers and four hundred and fifty men killed. Cumberland's Hanoverian Hussars, an entire regiment, having their Colonel Hacke at their head, who at a later date was tried and cashiered, turned bridle during the flight and fled into the forest of Soignies, spreading the rout as far as Brussels. The wagons, ammunition trains, baggage trains, & ambulance carts full of wounded, on seeing the French, gave ground, and approaching the forest, rushed into it; the

Dutch, sabered by the French cavalry, broke in confusion. From Vert Coucou to Groenendael, a distance of two leagues on the Brussels roads, there was, according to the testimony of living witnesses, a dense crowd of fugitives, and the panic was so great that it assailed the Prince de Conde at Mechlin and Louis XVIII. at Ghent ॐ With the exception of the weak reserve echelonned behind the field hospital established at the farm of Mont St. Jean, and Vivian's and Vandeleur's brigades, which flanked the left wing, Wellington had no cavalry left, and many of the guns lay dismounted ॐ These facts are confessed by Siborne, and Pringle, exaggerating the danger, goes so far as to state that the Anglo-Dutch army was reduced to thirty-four thousand men ॐ The Iron Duke remained firm, but his lips blanched. The Austrian commissioner Vincent, and the Spanish commissioner Alava, who were present at the battle, thought the Duke lost; at five o'clock Wellington looked at his watch, and could be heard muttering, "Blucher or night."

It was at this moment that a distant line of bayonets glistened on the heights on the side of Frischemont ✺ This was the climax of the gigantic drama.

Bulow to the Rescue

EVERYBODY knows Napoleon's awful mistake; Grouchy expected, and Blucher coming up, death instead of life ✺ Destiny has such turnings as this; men anticipate the throne of the world, and perceive St. Helena. If the little shepherd who served as guide to Bulow, Blucher's lieutenant, had advised him to debouch from the forest above Frischemont, instead of below Plancenoit, the form of the nineteenth century would have been different, for Napoleon would have won the battle of Waterloo. By any other road than that below Plancenoit the Prussian army would have come upon a ravine impassable, by artillery, & Bulow would not have arrived. ✺ Now one hour's delay—the Prussian general Muffling declares it—and Blucher would not have found Wellington erect.

—"The Battle was lost" ᔐ It was high time, as we see, for Bulow to arrive, and as it was he had been greatly delayed ᔐ He had bivouacked at Dieu-le-Mont and started at daybreak, but the roads were impracticable, and his division stuck in the mud. The ruts came up to the axletree of the guns; moreover, he was compelled to cross the Dyle by the narrow bridge of Wavre; the street leading to the bridge had been burnt by the French, & artillery train and limbers, which could not pass between the two rows of blazing houses, were compelled to wait till the fire was extinguished ᔐ By midday Bulow's vanguard had scarce reached Chapelle Saint Lambert.

Had the action begun two hours sooner, it would have been over at four o'clock, and Blucher would have fallen upon the battle gained by Napoleon. At midday, the emperor had been first to notice through his telescope on the extreme horizon, something which fixed his attention, and he said, "I see over there a cloud which appears to me to be troops." ᔐ Then he asked the Duke of Dalmatia, "Soult, what do you see in the direction of Chapelle

Saint Lambert?'' The marshal, after looking through his telescope, replied, ''Four
or five thousand men, sire.'' ✥ It was
evidently Grouchy, still they remained
motionless in the mist ✥ All the staff
examined the cloud pointed out by the
emperor, & some said, ''They are columns
halting,'' but the majority were of opinion
that they were trees ✥ The truth is that
the cloud did not move, and the emperor
detached Doncoul's division of light cavalry to reconnoiter in the direction of this
dark point.

Bulow, in fact, had not stirred, for his
vanguard was very weak and could effect
nothing. He was obliged to wait for the
main body of the army, and had orders
to concentrate his troops before forming
line; but at five o'clock, Blucher, seeing
Wellington's danger, ordered Bulow to attack, & employed the remarkable phrase,
''We must let the English army breathe.''
✥ A short time after, Losthin's, Hiller's
Hacke's, and Ryssel's brigades deployed
in front of Lobau's corps, the cavalry of
Prince William of Prussia debouched from
the Bois de Paris, Plancenoit was in flames,
& the Prussian cannon-balls began pouring

even upon the ranks of the guard held in reserve behind Napoleon.

The Guard

THE rest is known,—the irruption of a third army & the battle dislocated; eighty-six cannon thundering simultaneously; Pirch I. coming up with Bulow; Ziethen's cavalry led by Blucher in person; the French now driven back; Marcognet swept from the plateau of Ohain; Durutte dislodged from Papelotte; Donzelot & Quiot falling back; Lobau attacked on the flank; a new battle rushing at nightfall on the weakened French regiments; the whole English line resuming the offensive, and pushed forward; the gigantic gap made in the French army by the combined English & Prussian batteries; the extermination, the disaster in front, the disaster on the flank, and the guard forming line amid this fearful convulsion ❧ As they felt they were going to death, they shouted, "Long live the emperor!'' ❦ History has nothing more striking than this death-rattle breaking out into acclamations. The sky had been covered the whole day, but at this very moment, eight o'clock in the evening, the clouds parted in the horizon, and the sinister red glow of the setting sun was visible through the elms on the Nivelles road. It had been seen to rise at Austerlitz. ❡ Each battalion of the guard, for this denouement, was commanded by a general; Friant, Michel, Roguet, Harlot, Mallet, & Pont de Morvan, were there. When the tall bearskins of the Grenadiers of the Guard with the large eagle device appeared, symmetrical in line and calm, in the twilight of this fight, the enemy felt a respect for France; they fancied they saw twenty victories entering the battle-field with outstretched wings, and the men who were victors, esteeming themselves conquered, fell back; but Wellington shouted, "Up, guards, and take steady aim." The red regiment of English guards, which had been lying down behind the hedges, rose; a storm of canister rent the tricolor flag waving above the heads of the French; all rushed forward, and the supreme carnage commenced ❧ The imperial guard felt in the darkness the army giving way around them, and the vast staggering of the rout; they heard the cry of "*Sauve qui peut!*" substituted for the "*Vive l'empereur!*" & with flight behind them they continued to advance, hundreds falling at every step they took ❧ None hesitated or evinced timidity; the privates were as heroic as the generals, and not one attempted to escape suicide.

Ney, wild, and grand in the consciousness of accepted death, offered himself to every blow in this combat ❧ He had his fifth horse killed under him here ❧ Bathed in perspiration, with a flame in his eye, and foam on his lips, his uniform unbuttoned, one of his epaulettes half-cut through by the sabre-cut of a horse-guard, and his decoration of the great eagle dented by a bullet, — bleeding, muddy, magnificent, and holding a broken sword in his hand, he shouted, "Come & see how a marshal of France dies on the battle-field!" But it was in vain, he did not die ❧ He was haggard and indignant, and hurled at Drouet d'Erlon the question, "Are you not going to get yourself killed?" ❧ He yelled amid the roar of all this artillery, crushing a handful of men, "Oh! there is nothing for me! I should like all these English cannon-balls to enter my chest!" ❧ You were reserved for French bullets, unfortunate man.

The Catastrophe

THE rout in the rear of the guard was mournful; the army suddenly gave way on all sides simultaneously, at Hougomont, La Haye Sainte, Papelotte, & Plancenoit. The cry of "treachery" was followed by that of "*Sauve qui peut!*" ❧ An army which disbands is like a thaw,—all gives way, cracks, floats, rolls, falls, comes into collision, and dashes forward. Ney borrows a horse, leaps on it, & without hat, stock or sword, dashes across the Brussels road, stopping at once English and French. He tries to hold back the army, he recalls it, he insults it, he clings wildly to the rout to hold it back ❧ The soldiers fly from him, shouting, "Long live Marshal Ney!" Two regiments of Durotte's move backward & forward in terror, and as it were tossed between the sabres of the Hussars and the musketry fire of Kempt's, Best's and Pack's brigades. A rout is the highest of all confusions, for friends kill each other in order to escape, and squadrons & battalions dash against & destroy each other. Lobau at one extremity and Reille at the other are carried away by the torrent. In vain does Napoleon build a wall of what is left of the guard; in vain does he expend his own social squadrons in a final effort. ❧ Quiot retires before Vivian, Kellerman before Vandeleur, Lobau before Bulow, Moraud before Pirch, and Domor and Subervie before Prince William of Prussia. Guyot, who led the emperor's squadrons to the charge, falls beneath the horses of English dragoons. Napoleon gallops along the line of fugitives, harangues, urges, threatens & implores them; all the mouths that shouted "Long live the emperor" in the morning, remained wide open; they hardly knew him. The Prussian cavalry, who had come up fresh, dash forward, cut down, kill and exterminate. The artillery horses dash forward with the guns; the train soldiers unharness the horses from the caissons and escape on them; wagons overthrown and with their four wheels in the air, block up the road and supply opportunities for massacre ❧ Men crush each other and trample over the dead and over the living ❧ A multitude wild with terror fill the roads, the paths, the bridges, the plains, the hills, the valleys, and the woods, which are thronged by this flight of forty thousand men. Cries, desperation; knapsacks & muskets cast into the wheat; passages cut with the edge of the sabres; no comrades, no officers, no generals recognized — and indescribable terror ❧ Ziethen sabering France at his ease. The lions become kids ❧ Such was this fight.

¶ At Genappe, an effort was made to turn and rally ❧ Lobau collected three hundred men; the entrance of the village was barricaded, but at the first round of Prussian canister all began flying again, and Lobau was made prisoner. This shot may still be seen, buried in the gable of an old brick house on the right of the road, just before you reach Genappe. The Prussians dashed into Genappe, doubtless furious at being such small victors, and the pursuit was monstrous, for Blucher commanded extermination. Roguet had given the mournful example of threatening with death any French Grenadier who brought in a Prussian prisoner, & Blucher surpassed Roguet. Duchesme, general of the young guard, who was pursued into the doorway of an inn in Genappe, surrendered his sword to an Hussar of death, who took the sword & killed the prisoner. The victory was completed by the assassination of the vanquished. Let us punish as we are writing history, — old Blucher dishonored himself. This ferocity set the seal on the disaster; the desperate rout passed through Genappe, passed through Quatre Bras, passed through Sombreffe, passed through Frasnes, passed through Thuin, passed through Charleroi, & only stopped at the frontier ❧ Alas! and who was it flying in this way? The grand army. ❡ Did this vertigo, this terror, this overthrow of the greatest bravery that ever astonished history, take place without a cause? No. The shadow of a mighty right hand is cast over Waterloo; it is the day of destiny, and the force which is above man produced that day. Hence the terror, hence all those great souls laying down their swords. Those who had conquered Europe, fell crushed, having nothing more to say or do, and feeling a terrible presence in the shadow ❧ *Hoc erat in fatis.* On that day, the perspective of the human race was changed, and Waterloo is the hinge of the nineteenth century ❧ The disappearance of the great man was necessary for the advent of the great age, and He who cannot be answered undertook the task. The panic of the heroes admits of explanation; in the battle of Waterloo, there is more than a storm; there is a meteor ❧ ❧

At nightfall, Bernard and Bertrand seized by the skirt of his coat in a field near Genappe, a haggard, thoughtful, gloomy man, who, carried so far by the current of the rout, had just dismounted, passed the bridle over his arm, and was now, with wandering eye, returning alone to Waterloo ❧ It was Napoleon, the immense somnambulist of the shattered dream still striving to advance ❧ ❧ ❧ ❧

The Last Square

FEW squares of the guard, standing motionless in the swash of the rout, like rocks in running water, held out till night ◊ They awaited the double shadow of night and death, and let them surround them ◊ Each regiment, isolated from the others, and no longer connected with the army which was broken on all sides, died where it stood ◊ In order to perform this last exploit, they had taken up a position, some on the heights of Rossomme, others on the plain of Mont St. Jean ◊ The gloomy squares, deserted, conquered, and terrible, struggled formidably with death, for Ulm, Wagram, Jena, and Friedland were dying in it ◊ When twilight set in at nine in the evening, one square still remained at the foot of the plateau of Mont St. Jean ◊ In this mournful valley, at the foot of the slope scaled by the cuirassiers, now inundated by the English masses, beneath the converging fire of the

hostile and victorious artillery, under a
fearful hailstorm of projectiles, this square
still resisted. It was commanded by an obscure officer of the name of Cambronne.
᠅ At each volley the square diminished,
but continued to reply to the canister
with musketry fire, and each moment
contracted its four walls. Fugitives in the
distance, stopping at moments to draw
breath, listened in the darkness to this
gloomy diminishing thunder.
When this legion had become only a handful, when their colors were but a rag,
when their ammunition was exhausted,
and muskets were clubbed, and when the
pile of corpses was greater than the living
group, the victors felt a species of sacred
awe, & the English artillery ceased firing.
It was a sort of respite; these combatants
had around them an army of specters,
outlines of mounted men, the black profile of guns, and the white sky visible
through the wheels; the colossal death's
head which heroes ever glimpse in the
smoke of a battle, advanced and looked
at them. They could hear in the twilight
gloom that the guns were being loaded;
the lighted matches, resembling the eyes

of a tiger in the night, formed a circle round their heads ❧ The linstocks of the English batteries approached the guns, and at this moment an English general, Colville according to some, Maitland according to others, holding the supreme moment suspended over the heads of these men, shouted to them, "Brave Frenchmen, surrender!"

Cambronne answered, "Go to Hell!"

On hearing this insulting word, the English voice replied, "Fire!" The batteries belched forth flame, the hill trembled; from all these bronze throats issued a last and fearful eruption of canister; a vast smoke, whitened by the rising moon, rolled along the valley, and when it disappeared, there was nothing left ❧ This formidable remnant was annihilated, the guard was dead ❧ The four walls of the living redoubt were levelled with the ground; here and there a dying convulsion could be seen ❧ And it was thus that the French legions, greater than the Roman legions, expired at Mont St. Jean on the rain and blood-soaked ground, at the spot which Joseph, who carries the Nivelles mail-bags, now passes at four o'clock every morning, whistling and gaily flogging his horse.

Quot Libras in Dieu

THE battle of Waterloo is an enigma as obscure for those who gained it as for him who lost it. To Napoleon it is a panic; Blucher sees nothing in it but fire; Wellington does not understand it all. Look at the reports; the bulletins are confused; the commentaries are entangled; the latter stammer, the former stutter ꙮ Jomini divides the battle of Waterloo into four moments; Muffling cuts it into three acts; Charras, although we do not entirely agree with him in all his appreciations, has alone caught with his haughty eye the characteristic lineaments of this catastrophe of human genius contending with divine chance ꙮ All the other historians suffer from a certain bedazzlement in which they grope about. It was a flashing day, in truth the overthrow of the military monarchy which, to the great stupor of the kings, has dragged down all kingdoms, the downfall of strength and the rout of war.

In this event, which bears the stamp of superhuman necessity, men play but a small part; but if we take Waterloo from Wellington & Blucher, does that deprive England and Germany of anything? No. ✎ Neither illustrious England nor august Germany is in question in the problem of Waterloo, for thank heaven, nations are great without the mournful achievements of the sword ✎ Neither Germany, nor England nor France is held in a scabbard; at this day when Waterloo is only a clash of sabres, Germany has Goethe above Blucher, & England, Byron above Wellington. A mighty dawn of ideas is peculiar to our age, and in this dawn England and Germany have their own magnificent flash ✎ They are majestic because they think; the high level they bring to civilization is intrinsic to them; it comes from themselves and not from an accident. Any aggrandizement the nineteenth century may have cannot boast of Waterloo as its fountain head; for only barbarous nations grow suddenly after a victory—it is the transient vanity of torrents swollen by a storm. Civilized nations, especially at the present day, are not elevated or debased by the good or evil fortune of a captain, and their specific weight in the human family results from something more than a battle. Their honor, dignity, enlightenment, and genius, are not numbers which those gamblers, heroes and conquerors, can stake in the lottery of battles ❧ Very often a battle lost is progress gained, and less of glory more of liberty. The drummer is silent and reason speaks; it is the game of who loses wins ❧ Let us, then, speak of Waterloo coldly from both sides, & render to chance the things that belong to chance, and to God what is God's. What is Waterloo,—a victory? No; a quine in the lottery, won by Europe and paid by France; it was hardly worth while erecting a lion for it.

Waterloo, by the way, is the strangest encounter recorded in history; Napoleon and Wellington are not enemies, but contraries ❧ Never did God, who delights in antitheses, produce a more striking contrast or a more extraordinary confrontation. On one side precision, foresight,

90

geometry, prudence, a retreat assured, reserves prepared, an obstinate coolness, an imperturbable method, strategy profiting by the ground, tactics balancing battalions, carnage measured by a plumb-line, war regulated watch in hand, nothing left voluntarily to accident, old classic courage and absolute correctness ❧ On the other side we have intuition, divination, military strangeness, superhuman instinct, a flashing glance; something that gazes like the eagle and strikes like lightning, all the mysteries of a profound mind, association with destiny; the river, the plain, the forest and the hill summoned, and to some extent compelled to obey, the despot going so far as even to tyrannize over the battle-field; faith in a star blended with strategic science, heightening, but troubling it ❧ Wellington was the Bareme of war, Napoleon was its Michael Angelo, and this true genius was conquered by calculation. On both sides somebody was expected; and it was the exact-calculator who succeeded ❧ Napoleon waited for Grouchy, who did not come; Wellington waited for Blucher, and he came.

Wellington is the classical war taking its

revenge; Bonaparte, in his dawn, had met
it in Italy and superbly defeated it,—the
old owl fled before the young vulture ✎
The old tactics had been not only overthrown, but scandalized. Who was this
Corsican of six-and-twenty years of age?
What meant this splendid ignoramus who,
having everything against him, nothing
for him, without provisions, ammunition,
guns, shoes, almost without an army, with
a handful of men against masses, dashed
at allied Europe, & absurdly gained impossible victories? Who was this newcomer
of war who possessed the effrontery of a
planet? ✎ The academic military school
excommunicated him, while bolting, and
hence arose an implacable rancor of the
old Cæsarism against the new, of the old
sabre against the flashing sword, and of
the chess-board against genius. On June
18, 1815, this rancor got the best; and
beneath Lodi, Montebello, Montenotte,
Mantua, Marengo, and Arcola, it wrote,
—Waterloo. It was a triumph of medioc-
rity, sweet to majorities, and destiny
consented to this irony ✎ In his decline,
Napoleon found a young Suvarov before
him—in fact, it is only necessary to blanch

Wellington's hair in order to have a Suvarov ❧ Waterloo is a battle of the first class, gained by a captain of the second. ⁋ What must be admired in the battle of Waterloo is England, the English firmness, the English resolution, the English blood, & what England had really superb in it, is (without offense) herself; it is not her captain, but her army ❧ Wellington, strangely ungrateful, declares in his despatch to Lord Bathurst, that his army, the one which fought on June 18, 1815, was a "detestable army." What does the gloomy pile of bones buried in the trenches of Waterloo think of this? England has been too modest to herself in her treatment of Wellington, for making him so great is making herself small. Wellington is merely a hero like any other man ❧ The Scotch Greys, the Life Guards, Maitland & Mitchell's regiments, Pack & Kempt's infantry, Ponsonby and Somerset's cavalry, the Highlanders playing the bagpipes under the shower of canister, Ryland's battalions, the fresh recruits who could hardly manage a musket, & yet held their ground against the old bands of Essling & Rivoli —all this is grand. Wellington was tenacious, that was his merit, and we do not deny it to him, but the lowest of his privates and his troopers was quite as solid as he, and the iron soldier is as good as the iron duke. For our part all our glorification is offered to the English soldier, the English army, the English nation; and if there must be a trophy, it is to England that this trophy is owing. The Waterloo column would be more just, if, instead of the figure of a man, it raised to the clouds the statue of a people.

But this great England will be irritated by what we are writing here, for she still has feudal illusions, after her 1688, and the French 1789 ➣ This people believes in inheritance and hierarchy, and while no other excels it in power and glory, it esteems itself as a nation & not as a people. As a people, it readily subordinates itself, and takes a lord as its head, the workman lets himself be despised; the soldier puts up with flogging. It will be remembered that, at the battle of Inkermann, a sergeant who, it appears, saved the British army, could not be mentioned by Lord Raglan, because the military hierarchy does not allow any hero below the rank of officer to be mentioned in despatches. What we admire before all, in an encounter like Waterloo, is the prodigious skill of chance. The night rain, the wall of Hougomont, the hollow way of Ohain, Grouchy deaf to the cannon, Napoleon's guide deceiving him, Bulow's guide enlightening him—all this cataclysm is marvellously managed. ❡ Altogether, we will assert, there is more of a massacre than of a battle in Waterloo. Waterloo, of all pitched battles, is the one which had the smallest front for such a number of combatants ❧ Napoleon's, three-quarters of a league, Wellington's, half a league, and seventy-two thousand combatants on either side ❧ From this density came the carnage. The following calculation has been made and proportion established: Loss of men at Austerlitz, French, fourteen per cent; Russian, thirty per cent; Austrian, forty-four per cent; at Wagram, French, thirteen per cent; Austrian, fourteen per cent; at Moskova, French, thirty-seven per cent; Russian, forty-four per cent; at Bautzen, French, thirteen per cent; Russian and Prussian, fourteen per cent; at Waterloo, French, fifty-six per cent; Allies, thirty-one per cent;—total for Waterloo, forty-one per cent, or out of one hundred & forty-four thousand fighting men, sixty thousand killed ❧ ❧

The field of Waterloo has at the present day that calmness which belongs to the earth, & resembles all plains, but at night, a sort of visionary mist rises from it, and if any traveler walk about it, and listen and dream like Virgil on the mournful plain of Philippi, the hallucination of the catastrophe seizes upon him. The frightful June 18 lives again, the false monumental hill is levelled, the wondrous lion is dissipated, the battle-field resumes its reality, lines of infantry undulate on the plain, furious galloping crosses the horizon; the startled dreamer sees the flash of sabres, the sparkle of bayonets, the red light of shells, the monstrous collision of thunderbolts; he hears like a death-groan from the tomb, the vague clamor of the phantom battle ❧ These shadows are grenadiers; these flashes are cuirassiers; this skeleton is Napoleon; this skeleton is Wellington; all this is non-existent, and yet still combats, and the ravines are stained purple, and the trees rustle, & there is fury even in the clouds & in the darkness, while all the stern heights, Mont St. Jean, Hougomont, Frischemont, Papelotte, and Plancenoit, seem confusedly crowned by hosts of specters exterminating one another.

Ought We Applaud ?

THERE exists a highly respectable liberal school, which does not detest Waterloo, but we do not belong to it. For us Waterloo is only the stupefied date of liberty; for such an eagle to issue from such a shell is assuredly unexpected. ᴈ Waterloo, if we place ourselves at the culminating point of the question, is intentionally a counter-revolutionary victory, and it is Europe against France; it is Petersburg, Berlin, and Vienna against Paris; it is the *statu quo* opposed to the initiative; it is July 14, 1789, attacked through March 20, 1815; it is all the monarchies clearing the decks to conquer the indomitable French spirit of revolt. The dream was to extinguish this vast people which had been in a state of eruption for six-and-twenty years, and for this purpose, Brunswick, Nassau, the Romanoffs, Hohenzollern and the Hapsburger coalesced with the Bourbons, and Waterloo carries divine right on its pillion. It is true that as the empire was despotic, royalty, by the natural reaction of things, was compelled to be liberal, and a constitutional order issued from Waterloo, much to the regret of the conquerors. The fact is, that the Revolution can never be really conquered, and being providential & absolutely fatal, it constantly reappears, before Waterloo in Napoleon overthrowing the old thrones, after Waterloo in Louis XVIII. granting and enduring the charter. Bonaparte places a postillion on the throne of Naples, and a sergeant on the throne of Sweden, employing inequality to demonstrate equality; Louis XVIII. at St. Ouen countersigns the declaration of the rights of man. If you wish to understand what revolution is, call it progress; and if you wish to understand what progress is, call it to-morrow ❧ To-morrow ever does its work irresistibly and does it to-day, and it ever strangely attains its object ❧ It employs Wellington to make an orator of Foy who was only a soldier. Foy falls at Hougomont & raises himself in the tribune ❧ Such is the process of progress, and that workman has no bad tools; it fits to its divine work the man who bestrode the Alps and the old tottering patient of Pere Elysee, and it employs both the gouty man and the conqueror—the conqueror externally, the gouty man at home. Waterloo, by cutting short the demolition of thrones by the sword, had no other effect than to continue the revolutionary work on another side ❧ The sabres have finished, and the turn of the thinkers arrives; the age which Waterloo wished to arrest marched over it, & continued its route, and this sinister victory was gained by liberty.

Still it is incontestable that what triumphed at Waterloo; what smiled behind Wellington; what procured him all the marshals' staffs of Europe, including, by the way, that of marshal of France; what rolled along joyously the wheelbarrows of earth mingled with bones, to erect the foundation for the lion, on whose pedestal is inscribed the date, June 18, 1815; what encouraged Blucher in cutting down the routed army; and what from the plateau of Mont St. Jean hovered over France like a prey,—was the counter-revolution. It is the counter-revolution that muttered the hideous word, "dismemberment," but on reaching Paris it had a close view of the crater, it felt that the ashes burnt its feet, and it reflected. It went back to the job of stammering a charter. ❡ Let us only see in Waterloo what there really is in it There is no intentional liberty, for the counter-revolution was involuntarily liberal in the same way as Napoleon, through a corresponding phenomenon, was involuntarily a Revolutionist ❧ On June 18, 1815, Robespierre on horseback was thrown ❧

Divine Right Restored

WITH the fall of the dictatorship, an entire European system crumbled away, and the empire vanished in a shadow which resembled that of the expiring Roman world. Nations escaped from the abyss as in the time of the barbarians, but the barbarism of 1815, which could be called by its familiar name, the counter-revolution, had but little breath, soon began to pant, and stopped ✎ The empire, we confess, was lamented and by heroic eyes, & its glory consists in the sword-made scepter,—the empire was glory itself. It had spread over the whole earth all the light that tyranny can give—a dim light, we will say, an obscure light, for when compared with real day, it is night. This disappearance of the night produced the effect of an eclipse. ⁋ Louis XVIII. re-entered Paris, and the dances of July 8, effaced the enthusiasm of March 20 ✎ The Corsican became the antithesis of the Bearnais, and the flag on the dome of the Tuileries was white ❧ The exile was enthroned, and the deal table of Hartwell was placed before the easy chair of Louis XIV. People talked of Bouvines & Fontenoy as if they occurred only yesterday, while Austerlitz was antiquated. The throne and the altar fraternized majestically, and one of the most indubitable forms of the welfare of society in the nineteenth century was established in France and on the continent—Europe took the white cockade. Trestaillon was celebrated, and the motto, "*Nec pluribus impar*" reappeared in the stone beams representing a sun on the front of the barracks, on the Quai d'Orsay ❧ Where there had been an imperial guard, there was a "red household;" & the arch of the Carrousel, if loaded with badly endured victories, feeling not at home in these novelties, and perhaps slightly ashamed of Marengo and Arcola, got out of the difficulty by accepting the statue of the Duc d'Angouleme. The cemetery of the Madeleine, a formidable public grave in 1793, was covered with marble and jasper, because the bones of Louis XVI. & Marie Antoinette were mingled with that dust.

In the moat of Vincennes a tomb emerged from the ground, as a reminder that the Duc d'Enghien died there in the same month in which Napoleon was crowned. Pope Pius VII. who had performed the ceremony very close upon that death, tranquilly blessed the downfall, as he had blessed the elevation ❧ There was at Schonbrunn a shadow four years of age, whom it was seditious to call the king of Rome. And these things took place, and these kings regained their thrones, and the master of Europe was put in a cage, and the old regime became the new, and the light and the shadow of the earth changed places, because on the afternoon of a summer day, a peasant boy said to a Prussian in a wood, "Go this way and not that!"

That 1815 was a sort of melancholy April; the old unhealthy and venomous realities assumed a new aspect. Falsehood espoused 1789, divine right put on the mask of a charter; fictions became constitutional; prejudices, superstitions & afterthoughts having article fourteen in their hearts, var-nished themselves with liberalism ❧ The snakes cast their slough. Man had been at once aggrandized and lessened by Napoleon; idealism, in this reign of splendid materialism, received the strange name of ideology. It was a grave imprudence of a great man to ridicule the future, but the people, that food for powder, so amorous of gunners, sought him ❧ "Where is he? What is he doing?" "Napoleon is dead," said a passer-by to an invalid of Marengo and Waterloo ❧ "He dead!" the soldier exclaimed; "Much you know about him!" ❧ Imaginations defied this thrown man. Europe after Waterloo was dark, for some enormous gap was long left unfilled after the disappearance of Napoleon. The kings placed themselves in this gap, and old Europe took advantage of it to effect a reformation. There was a holy alliance — Belle Alliance, the fatal field of Waterloo had said beforehand ❧ In the presence of the old Europe reconstituted, the lineaments of a new France were sketched in. The future, derided by the emperor, made its entry and wore on its brow the star—Liberty. The ardent eyes of the youthful generation were turned toward it, but, singular to say, they simultaneously felt equally attached to this future liberty and to the past Napoleon. ❧ Defeat had made the conquered man greater; Napoleon fallen seemed better than Napoleon standing on his feet ❧ Those who had triumphed were alarmed. ❧ England had him guarded by Hudson Lowe, and France had him watched by Montcheme ❧ His folded arms became the anxiety of thrones, and Alexander christened him his nightmare. This terror resulted from the immense amount of revolution he had in him, and it is this which explains and excuses Bonapartistic liberalism. This phantom caused the old world to tremble, and kings sat uneasily on their throne, with the rock of St. Helena on the horizon ❧ ❧

While Napoleon was dying at Longwood, the sixty thousand men who fell at Waterloo rotted calmly, and something of their peace spread over the world. The congress of Vienna converted it into the treaties of 1815, & Europe called that the Restoration. ❡ Such is Waterloo, but what does the Infinite care? All this tempest, all this cloud, this war, & then this peace; all this shadow did not for a moment disturb the flash of that mighty eye before which a spider, leaping from one blade of grass to another, equals the eagle flying from tower to tower at Notre Dame.